# Before Ever After

Tangled
The Series

Before Ever After

Retold by Stacia Deutsch

Random House 🏠 New York

randomhousekids.com

ISBN 978-0-7364-3824-7 (hardcover)
Printed in the United States of America
10 9 8 7 6 5 4 3

Random House Children's Books supports
the First Amendment and celebrates the right to read.

# Before Ever After

chapter

1

Two horses galloped over rugged terrain, past large rocks and tall trees. Rapunzel rode on Fidella, a strong brown mare, while Eugene rode Maximus. Max's white coat glimmered in the shadows of the forest.

"They're gaining on us!" Rapunzel shouted to Eugene. Her heart raced as she quickly peeked over her shoulder. "There are more of them," she reported.

"Good. It'll keep things interesting," Eugene replied, his voice calm and steady. Max kept pace with Fidella, but the soldiers were still on their heels. "Man, these guys are persistent."

"So am I," Rapunzel said. "I'll meet you at the wall." She flashed Eugene a rebellious look and spurred her horse ahead.

"Sounds like a challenge." Eugene raised an eyebrow as Rapunzel took the high path. He stayed low, moving quickly into the valley.

"Think you can keep up?" she teased.

"Oh, it's not me you have to worry about." Eugene gave her a charming grin, then directed her attention to the horses that were gaining on Fidella.

"Uh-oh," Rapunzel gasped. The soldiers were moving fast.

"They're your problem now." Eugene turned his horse away as the guards took off after Rapunzel. Unfortunately, his freedom didn't last long.

"Oh, great," he muttered. Two guards had broken from the pack and were now following him. The larger one with the dark mustache was closing in. This was the big boss, the captain of the royal guard, and he was an excellent horseman. The

4

second guard wasn't too shabby a rider, either. He was still a little ways back but was gaining.

"Okay, Max, follow my lead," Eugene said.

Max whinnied cheerfully. He loved a game of chase as much as Eugene.

But Eugene's plan immediately changed when he noticed danger ahead. "Oh . . . log, log, log, log!" A rotten trunk from a fallen tree blocked their path. The trunk was lying across a narrow opening, like a low bridge. If Eugene smacked into it, he had no doubt the log would throw him to the ground.

Once enemies, Max and Eugene were now so close they could read each other's minds. Max neighed a warning as he ducked under the log. Eugene got the message, and in that same moment, he jumped over the log and landed perfectly on Max's back on the other side. They never even slowed down.

The captain of the guard saw how Eugene handled the obstacle and executed the exact same maneuver. He went over the log, the horse went under, and moments later, they were back to chasing Eugene.

The younger guard was not as lucky. He jumped over the log and his horse went under, but he missed the horse's back and landed in a mud puddle instead.

"Oooh, good thing his face broke his fall," Eugene joked before turning his attention ahead.

Meanwhile, Rapunzel was riding on the upper trail. Her short brown hair blew in the wind as she galloped at high speed.

Her hair hadn't always been this short—or this brown. It used to be seventy feet long, blond, and enchanted. When her mother, the queen, was pregnant with Rapunzel, the queen became very ill. A magical sundrop flower brought the queen back to health, and when the princess was born, the magic lived on in Rapunzel's hair.

When Rapunzel was a baby, evil Mother Gothel stole her away. She wanted the golden flower's

6

magic for herself and tricked Rapunzel into believing that she was her true mother. For eighteen years, she kept Rapunzel locked in a tower and used her hair's magic to stay young. And for each of those years, the kingdom mourned their lost princess.

Eugene helped Rapunzel escape the tower prison and took her to see the floating lanterns the kingdom released every year on the lost princess's birthday. At the time, they didn't know that those lanterns were for Rapunzel.

Back then, Eugene was a thief who called himself Flynn Rider. But Rapunzel chose to call him by his real name: Eugene Fitzherbert.

When Mother Gothel tried to kill Eugene, Rapunzel healed him with the flower's magic. He then cut Rapunzel's hair, destroying the magic forever. He did this to protect her from Mother Gothel. Without the magic of Rapunzel's hair, Mother Gothel soon turned to dust.

The rest was history. Rapunzel was reunited

with her parents, the king and queen of Corona. She and Eugene moved into the castle, and through it all, they fell in love.

They planned to get married . . . eventually.

But marriage, family, and ruling Corona would all come later.

At this moment, Rapunzel had only one goal in mind: she was going to win the race and beat Eugene to the kingdom wall!

A chameleon named Pascal clung to Rapunzel's shoulder. When Rapunzel was trapped in Mother Gothel's tower, Pascal had been her only friend. He had been by her side ever since.

As Fidella galloped, Pascal gripped Rapunzel tightly. He clicked his tongue to report on the guards who were chasing them.

There was only one man left to outrun. Rapunzel was confident they'd get away. "Whoa!" she suddenly exclaimed. In a flash, she pulled on her horse's reins, warning, "Bunny crossing. Careful, Fidella."

Hundreds of bunnies were on the path. Fidella

danced and dodged around the little creatures.

"Watch out," Rapunzel said as she expertly guided her horse through the warren. "Cute little bunnies."

They made it safely through, but the castle guard who was behind them got stuck in a mountain of bunnies.

Pascal snickered and waved goodbye to the guard while Fidella plunged forward toward Eugene, Max, and their meeting place.

Eugene, however, was still in trouble.

"You're not getting away this time!" the captain shouted as he moved in on Eugene and Max. He reached toward Eugene.

With a mighty "Hi-ya!" Rapunzel and Fidella leaped into the small space between Max and the captain's horse. The guard had to pull back so as not to crash.

"Sorry!" she called over her shoulder as they galloped away. Then she turned to Eugene and broke into a grin. "We're almost there!"

But again, their freedom didn't last long.

Eugene glanced behind them. "Oh, come on!" he moaned. The captain of the guard was speeding their way.

Rapunzel looked at the guard, then at a deep ravine ahead. She knew they could make it across and urged Fidella to go faster. Eugene and Max followed her lead. They hit the edge of the ravine and the horses leaped toward the other end, landing comfortably on the far side.

The captain's horse followed but landed on a fallen log rather than the hard ground. Max gave the log a push with his back legs as he hurried away, tipping the guard and his horse into the river below.

Finally, the chase was over!

Rapunzel rode on, but Eugene took a minute to turn Max around and watch the captain climb out of the water, dripping wet. His steed was soaked, too.

"Looking good, Cap," Eugene said with a satisfied smile, then went after Rapunzel.

Rapunzel felt confident that no one else was chasing her when she reached the giant wall that surrounded the kingdom. She reined in Fidella at the spot where the famous sun symbol of Corona was painted on the wall. The horse instinctively knew what she wanted. Raising her front hooves, Fidella gave her rider a boost.

Pulling herself up the last few inches, Rapunzel stood on the broad, high wall. She basked in the early-morning sunlight, arms outstretched, taking it all in. The valley spread out before her, with glistening rivers and majestic mountains in brilliant shades of gold, purple, blue, red, and green.

Pascal was still on her shoulder, sharing the moment. This was the world beyond the safe walls of Corona. Rapunzel was certain she felt her heart skip a beat.

"Oh, Pascal, look at that view!" she exclaimed.

After being trapped in a tower her whole life, Rapunzel was amazed at all the mysteries the world held.

Eugene arrived with a loud "Ha ha!" He leaped toward Rapunzel but didn't quite make it. He caught the wall's edge and pulled himself up next to her.

"Okay, okay, I know what you're thinking," he started. "It may have seemed like you won, but you've got to take into account that my hair is actually longer than yours now, so we have to factor in wind resistance." He ran his hands through his hair and flipped it a few times.

"Hmm." Rapunzel didn't argue. She smiled and turned her attention back to the view. "Have you ever seen anything so beautiful?" she asked.

Eugene turned to look at her. He reached out and took her hand in his, and said, "Yes, yes, I have."

Rapunzel knew he was talking about her. She turned toward him, her heart full. For a long moment, they stared into each other's eyes. This was true love.

They moved slowly, leaning in for a kiss, only to be interrupted by the *clip-clop* of horse hooves.

"The game's over, Your Highness." It was the captain of the guard, dripping wet and clearly annoyed. He needed Eugene and Rapunzel to return to the castle immediately. "The welcoming ceremony is about to begin." Their friendly game of chase was officially over.

Eugene pulled back. "Well, I suppose we showed them who's boss." He put a hand on his hip. "So how about we go and make you an official princess?"

Rapunzel gave him a teasing grin. "Oh, is that *today*?"

Eugene chuckled. "Very funny. Come on. We'd better get you back to the castle." He lowered himself down the wall, then paused. "Oooh, maybe I can squeeze in a royal massage—before my daily trim, of course." Unlike Rapunzel, Eugene was having no difficulty settling in to the comforts of castle life. The more pampering, the better. He dropped to the ground.

Pascal drew Rapunzel's attention to the world beyond the wall. She nodded, understanding exactly what he meant. "I know, Pascal," she said, glancing wistfully at the view. "We'll get out there soon." Then she leaped off the wall, mounted Fidella, and spurred her horse ahead, calling over her shoulder to Eugene, "Race you back to the castle!"

They were off.

The captain put his head in his hands and sighed. Would those two ever behave like true royals?

chapter

2

The village square was buzzing with excitement as Rapunzel and Eugene passed through on their way to the castle. Everyone was getting ready for the princess's big weekend. Coronation announcements were being posted, and banners and decorations were being put up.

Throughout town, people hung the same kind of lanterns that were released on Rapunzel's birthday every year. Rapunzel couldn't help smiling, remembering how the lanterns connected her to her family. Now she was here—reunited with her mother and father and living a happily-ever-after life.

She and Eugene reached the castle courtyard to

find her good friend Cassandra waiting for them. Cassandra's dark eyes and short black hair made her easy to spot. But Cassandra was more than a friend—she was also Rapunzel's lady-in-waiting, and her father was the captain of the guard. She'd been alerted that Rapunzel and Eugene were on their way back and was ready to escort Rapunzel to her room. It was time to get her dressed for the first coronation event—dinner with royal guests.

They were running late, but Eugene still took the opportunity to be a gentleman and help Rapunzel off her horse. Rapunzel leaned in to kiss him, but Cassandra quickly interrupted, dragging the soon-to-be-official-princess off to get ready.

Max gave Eugene a nice horsey kiss instead. Eugene immediately wiped his face and moved out of range in case he tried again.

As Cassandra led Rapunzel through the village to the castle, the princess tried her best to do the things a princess was supposed to do. But all these royal duties were completely new to

18

her. Thankfully, Cassandra let her know when it was time to curtsy to people or respond to staff. When Rapunzel stopped to accept a flower from a young girl, Cassandra tugged her forward, calling, "Princess, the time!" Rapunzel frowned.

Once inside the castle, it was Cassandra's turn to frown when she saw that Rapunzel's bare feet had left muddy prints down the hall. Rapunzel didn't like shoes. She'd gone so long without them, why did she need them now? She liked feeling the grass beneath her feet, dipping her toes in a nearby puddle, or sliding across the newly polished castle floor. Life was more exciting without shoes.

But in general, Rapunzel didn't really understand the clothing required of her. All her life she had worn the same simple purple dress. Now she had dresses for every occasion. They often involved corsets, buckles, and bows that were complicated and uncomfortable. Today she was supposed to wear a long pink dress with a cream petticoat, a dark pink bodice, and a high collar.

Then there were the names of all the staff and important dignitaries to remember. She constantly messed those up.

Yet Rapunzel didn't complain. After all, this was her happily-ever-after.

When they reached Rapunzel's bedroom, the handmaidens swooped in to help her change outfits. But when they started making too many demands, Cassandra shooed them away.

"That's enough. I'll take it from here." The women moved back and gave the girls space. "How are you holding up?" Cassandra asked Rapunzel.

"Busy," Rapunzel said as she let out a sigh. "But busy is good!" She tried to sound upbeat.

"I'm glad you think so, Raps," Cassandra said, "because this welcoming ceremony is just the beginning. Tomorrow's the festival, followed by the royal banquet. And that's all before the actual coronation on Sunday—" She stopped mid-sentence when she noticed Rapunzel's still-bare feet. "Oh, come on, really?"

Rapunzel grinned sheepishly. Pascal peeked

over her shoulder as Cassandra tugged down on the gown to hide her toes.

Cassandra softened. "Look, Rapunzel. I know this princess thing is new to you, but you've got to at least try to act the part."

"Trust me, Cassandra," Rapunzel replied as they stepped in front of the king's portrait, "I know how important this is to my dad." She gave the painting a loving look.

While Cassandra and Rapunzel finished getting ready, King Frederic was in a meeting room with one of his advisors. The captain of the guard was showing him a map of the castle grounds. The king stood with his jeweled crown perched atop his head.

"As you requested, Your Majesty, we've doubled security on both the main gates and the south towers," the captain said, indicating the places on the map.

"Good," the king replied. "We're expecting guests from all over the world. I want them to know that they are safe." He opened the doors of the room. "Everything for my little girl's coronation weekend *must* be absolutely perfect." He walked into the hallway and headed toward Rapunzel's room. He smiled when he saw the girls.

Cassandra curtsied while Rapunzel greeted her father. "Hi, Dad."

King Frederic had missed Rapunzel terribly during the years she'd been missing. Now that she was back, he wouldn't let anything happen to her again. He would use all his resources to protect her.

The king swept Rapunzel into a tight hug. When they stepped apart, he looked at her in earnest and said, "Now, as princess, you're representing not only yourself and the family, but all of Corona."

"Don't worry, Dad. I won't let you down," Rapunzel assured him. "Listen, while we're on the whole coronation thingy . . . These royal activities are great, but do you think I might be able to have a little downtime soon?"

King Frederic reached out and took Rapunzel's hands. "I know this is new, but you'll adjust."

He kissed her on the head. "After all, your *friend* seems to be getting on just fine."

Her *friend*—Eugene—really was having a grand time, soaking up everything royal life had to offer. While Rapunzel and Cassandra were getting ready, Eugene was happily picking his outfits for the coronation weekend.

Max and the pub thugs were hanging out in Eugene's room as stylists dressed him. The pub thugs consisted of: Hook Foot, a budding dancer; Big Nose, a hopeless romantic; Vladimir, the strongest of the bunch; Attila, a baker at heart; Shorty, the oldest of the group; and Ulf, a mime. An odd bunch of former thieves, the thugs looked scarier than they actually were. They were all at the castle for Rapunzel's big weekend.

When Eugene and Rapunzel had met the pub thugs, back when the couple had first escaped the tower, the thugs had wanted to capture Eugene because there was a hefty reward on his head. But after Rapunzel told them her dream of seeing the floating lights, and how Eugene had promised to help her, they had shared their own dreams and the two groups quickly became friends. Now they all stood around watching while a castle stylist, Hermut, put a tacky hat on Eugene.

"Oooh. Hermut, my man, this hat ties the whole outfit together," said Eugene. "I know what you're all thinking: Why is Eugene in such a good mood today? I mean, what gives?"

The pub thugs looked at one another. That was *not* what they were thinking.

Eugene went on, telling them his grand plans. At the royal banquet tomorrow, he would give Rapunzel a rose and then get down on one knee and ask her to marry him. He showed his friends the sparkly diamond ring he would give her. They were excited, especially Big Nose, the romantic of the group.

Eugene knew the banquet would be the perfect moment to carry out his plan. "Life's gonna be like strawberry sherbet once she's Mrs. Eugene

Fitzherbert!" It wasn't the best rhyme, so he changed it to "Once she's *Princess* Eugene Fitzherbert." Eugene stared at the glistening ring he'd chosen. He and Rapunzel would finally be together and live their own happily-ever-after.

What Eugene didn't understand was that he and Rapunzel had different ideas of what "happily ever after" meant. Before meeting Rapunzel, Eugene had spent his whole life on the road. He was ready to settle down now. Rapunzel, on the other hand, had never seen the world. That was what she wanted most.

While Eugene continued getting dressed and making plans, Rapunzel was back in her room, thinking about her own plans.

As she absentmindedly spun a globe, questions flooded her mind. What did this new future look like? Could she handle all the requirements that came with being a princess? Was this royal life happily ever after? It felt as if the adventure she and Eugene had had together was coming to an end, and this new life seemed so overwhelming.

In his room, Eugene tucked the engagement ring into his pocket, while in her room, Rapunzel picked up her crown. "Okay, no pressure. Just introducing myself to the most important people in the world. Representing my mom, my dad, and the entire kingdom." She took a deep breath and looked in the mirror confidently. "We've got this," she told herself, hoping it was true.

Outside the castle, the streets of Corona were buzzing with welcoming-ceremony preparations. Everyone was thrilled at the princess's return and couldn't wait to celebrate alongside her and her family. A young boy posted coronation announcements on a cobblestone wall. He didn't notice when a rat stole one and escaped into the sewer, holding the announcement firmly in its jaws.

Deep in the underground world of the sewer, the rat approached a woman, her face covered by shadows, and delivered the announcement to her.

Nearby, several thieves were counting recently stolen loot.

One of the thieves addressed the woman. "My Lady Kane. What is it?"

Lady Kane read the piece of paper. "Time to pay our respects to our beloved royals," she said with a satisfied smirk. Then she lit the coronation announcement on fire and watched it burn to ash.

At the castle's main entrance, the royal family stood together to welcome their guests. Rapunzel's mother had long brown hair and kind eyes. She waited calmly next to her daughter. Rapunzel tried to mimic her. She stared nervously at the long drive, where carriages holding dignitaries were arriving.

"We're good at making people feel welcome," Rapunzel whispered to Pascal. "This is completely doable-ish." She was more worried than she let on.

Looking toward the crowd, Rapunzel caught

Eugene's eye. He was wearing a new outfit and waving wildly. She smiled, comforted to know he was nearby. But when she waved back, her father cleared his throat, reminding her to act more noble.

"Your Highness, I present Dame Elizabeth Van Hoskins of Rochester," a footman announced, opening a carriage door for the first guest.

Rapunzel lunged at the woman, giving her a huge bear hug. "Get in here," she said, hugging the woman tighter. Dame Elizabeth looked up in shock. "So nice to meet you!" Rapunzel said, stepping back and straightening the lady's fancy hat.

Pascal cringed.

Eugene grimaced.

The king sighed. "Uh, perhaps you should refrain from the bear hugs, sweetheart," he whispered.

Rapunzel recognized her mistake. "Oh. No bear hugs. Gotcha. Sorry."

Next, a stone-faced man in a decorated military uniform arrived. He stepped out of the carriage as the footman proclaimed, "I present Lieutenant Commander General James Rutherford-Carver the Third."

"Phew. That's a mouthful," Rapunzel said to the lieutenant. "Is it okay if I call you Jimmy?"

"I'd prefer you didn't," the man said, unamused, and walked away.

"Well, welcome all the same," Rapunzel called after him with a small wave.

She turned to the third arriving carriage. When the door opened, there stood the epitome of regalness: a beautiful young woman wearing an enormous Victorian wig.

"The Duchess of Quintonia," the footman announced.

The duchess fluttered her ornate fan.

"Wow," Rapunzel started. "Can I just say I *love* your hair? I used to have really long hair too, but—"

The duchess interrupted, speaking in a formal tone. "*This* is a handwoven coiffure made from the finest silk and Vacuna fabrics. It designates high social status." She paused, then added cattily, "I'd think *you'd* know that."

Rapunzel stared at the girl, stunned, uncertain whether she'd been insulted. "Still. Nice to m-meet you," she stammered.

Snickering, the duchess pointed at Rapunzel's bare feet. "Sadly, not nice enough to wear shoes, I'm afraid."

Rapunzel tried to hide her toes, but it was too late. Heat rose to her face—could she get nothing right today? Queen Arianna put a supportive hand on Rapunzel's shoulder while Pascal gave her a sympathetic look.

Once again, she apologized to her father, whispering a small "Sorry."

chapter

3

At the end of the evening, Rapunzel escaped to the harbor. She felt as if she had messed up her princess duties once again. There was so much she didn't understand about royal life. She just needed a few minutes alone. At the dock, she climbed into a gondola tethered to the shore, stared into the water, and sighed. Thousands of tiny stars reflected back at her.

Suddenly, Eugene's face was in the water next to hers. Rapunzel turned to find him behind her.

"So," he said. "I think we learned something valuable today: there's a time and place for bear hugs." He studied Rapunzel for a beat. She was curled up in the boat, her arms wrapped around her bent knees. "Hey, you okay?" he asked, jumping in beside her.

"Yeah, great. Why wouldn't I be?" she said. But she was unsure. It had been a rough day, and she felt conflicted about her new role. She gave him a long look, then asked, "Eugene, is all this everything you dreamed it would be?" She gestured to the castle glowing in the moonlight.

"Rapunzel, you are my dream," he replied honestly, taking her hand in his. "So as long as you're with me, the answer's always going to be yes." He returned her look, studying her face. "Don't you feel the same way?"

"No!" she blurted out. Wait, that wasn't what she meant. "Yes!" she corrected herself. But that wasn't it, either. "I mean, of course I do. I love you with all my heart, Eugene." She held his hand against her face.

"Look," Eugene said. "I know this has to be weird." He followed her gaze up and over his

34

shoulder toward the castle. "No one's expecting you to take it all in overnight, but believe me, I've been all around the world and it doesn't get any better than this. The castle, our friends, your family, *each other* . . . what else could you possibly want?"

Rapunzel didn't answer right away. Instead she stared out into the distance, past the castle, past the wall of Corona. Then she turned back to find Eugene gazing at her with hopeful, loving eyes. She couldn't find the words to voice what she felt inside, so she simply answered, "Nothing."

They leaned in for a kiss just as Cassandra appeared at the dock. "Time to go!" she called in a loud voice.

Rapunzel and Eugene were so startled that Eugene fell out of the gondola and landed in the water with a mighty splash.

"GAH!" He grabbed the side of the boat and came to the surface spitting water.

"How's that water feel, Fitzherbert?" Cassandra

35

asked with a chuckle. Eugene and Cassandra were always joking around. Even though they hadn't known each other that long, it felt like they'd been friends forever.

Eugene glared up at Cassandra from the side of the boat. "Dark," he replied. "And icy . . . just like you."

Cassandra chuckled again, then turned to Rapunzel. "Come on. It's time to head in. You don't want to be exhausted for tomorrow."

At that, Rapunzel's eyes lit up. "Right! My morning off!"

Rapunzel helped Eugene into the boat and gave him a quick kiss on the forehead. "Sorry," she said.

The two girls walked away while Eugene wrung out his wet hair.

The next day, the town square was bustling with activity. Trumpets blared and castle guards lined up for duty.

"The Princess Rapunzel will spend her day about town!" the trumpeter declared to the villagers.

The crowd cheered.

Rapunzel couldn't wait to mingle with the people. The guards moved aside to allow her to pass through but then closed ranks. She tried to wave to the crowd but was blocked by her protection squad. They were determined to keep her safe.

Rapunzel spotted a vendor raising a cleaver to cut a large ham. He was instantly attacked by several guardsmen. Thinking he could harm the princess, the guards knocked him down and forcibly removed the "weapon" from his hand.

Rapunzel cringed. On her shoulder, Pascal was appalled.

They moved farther into the square, where Rapunzel was thrilled to see a long line of well-wishers. The people extended their hands toward her in greeting. But each time someone reached forward, a guard knocked their hand back with an audible slap. *Slap, slap, slap.* The guards wouldn't allow anyone to get too close to the princess.

Rapunzel cringed again, and Pascal furrowed his brow.

When a fire juggler wanted to put on a show for her, she waited with anticipation. A giant flame burst from each of the juggler's torches, but before he could continue the show, the guards doused him with water. Fire juggling was too dangerous in the guards' minds.

Next, they passed an enormous prized pig with giant tusks. Rapunzel headed toward the attraction but was stopped by a guard. He handed her a balloon that looked like a pig instead. It immediately popped! Thinking the loud noise meant danger, the guards jumped into action, surrounding Rapunzel with weapons as if preparing for battle.

The overprotection didn't stop there. At the fountain in the center of town were some familiar faces. Four young girls sat in a row braiding one another's hair. They were the same girls who had

helped Rapunzel braid her hair when she had first come to Corona. She wanted nothing more than to go play with them, but a guard took her place and roughly braided the oldest girl's hair while Rapunzel and Pascal sat a safe distance away, watching helplessly.

Rapunzel was feeling increasingly annoyed. She thought a cupcake might cheer her up, so she headed to the baker, who offered her a beautiful treat with a cherry on top. She reached out, but a guard intercepted. He took the cupcake, sniffed it, stuck his finger down the middle, and smashed it all around. When he decided it was safe, he handed the crumbs to Rapunzel. She looked at Pascal and they agreed—the great day she'd hoped for was ruined.

Back in her room, Rapunzel sat on her bed feeling tired and frustrated. Cassandra noticed her bad mood. "Let me guess," she said. "Your big day on the town wasn't all you hoped it would be?"

Rapunzel sighed, choosing her words carefully. "It was *interesting.*"

Pascal was far more honest, sticking out his tongue and giving the morning a big chameleon thumbs-down.

"Uh-huh," Cassandra replied. "I bet."

"I just wish my dad would let me get out and see the real world," Rapunzel said.

Cassandra pushed open the window. "You know," she said, "if you really wanted, I could get you in and out of here before anyone even knew we were gone."

Pascal squeaked with excitement.

Rapunzel couldn't believe it was possible. "You mean *sneak me* out?"

"Exactly," Cassandra said. "What you do when no one's looking is your business."

Rapunzel had never considered that idea before. Suddenly, a knock at the door interrupted her thoughts.

"The royal banquet is ready to receive the princess now," a voice called.

*Another princess duty already?* Rapunzel sighed.

Cassandra smiled at Rapunzel's expression. "Cheer up, Raps. Hey, maybe your dad got someone to chew your food for you," she joked.

Rapunzel didn't laugh. They headed to the hall.

The royal banquet was noisy. People from around the kingdom gathered to celebrate with Rapunzel and her family. Rapunzel quickly found her seat between her parents at the royal table.

Nearby, Eugene took a long, secretive look at the engagement ring he had picked. He tucked it away in his pocket, and then, a mere second later, he was hit with flying food and surrounded by a rambunctious group of kids. *Why did the king put me at the kids' table? Is this some kind of joke?* he wondered.

But it hadn't been the king.

"I'm in charge of the seating charts," Cassandra

said as she passed by. "It's one of the perks of the job." She smiled.

Eugene glared at her. Yet he couldn't be angry. He wouldn't let anything ruin his plans.

Rapunzel, on the other hand, was clearly not happy. She sat picking at her food, not eating much. Her crown sparkled on her short brown hair.

The king turned to her. "I don't understand why you're upset, sweetheart. I said you could do whatever you wanted today, and that is exactly what you did."

"You didn't say anything about a battalion tagging along," Rapunzel replied softly so no one would overhear her complaint.

"Why would I need to?" The king didn't understand. "You're royalty making a public appearance."

"But, Dad—" Rapunzel began to protest but was interrupted.

Eugene tapped his glass and stepped to the center of the banquet room. "Ladies and gentlemen, dukes and duchesses, barons and baronesses, marquesses and, you know, the female version of those . . . may I share a moment of history with you?" He reached toward Rapunzel. "Princess? Would you join me?"

Rapunzel got up from the table, and she and Eugene stood before all the guests. *What's going on?* she wondered. Her frustration with her father shifted to confusion. She glanced past Eugene toward Cassandra, looking for answers. Cassandra shrugged—she didn't know what was going on, either.

"Tonight, we celebrate our love for the princess. I, for one, can think of no better way to celebrate the love I have for her than this." Eugene lowered to one knee before Rapunzel, ready to propose.

"Oh, Eugene." Rapunzel looked around, still not understanding. "Wait. Did you drop something?"

Eugene whispered, "No," then pulled the ring box from his pocket. He opened it to show her the beautiful, twinkling diamond engagement ring he'd picked just for her.

The crowd gasped. The king leaped to his feet.

"Rapunzel, from the moment I first met you and you knocked me out with that frying pan, I knew it was love," Eugene said. "You're my life. You're my best friend. And I want to be your partner in all things."

Rapunzel smiled. This was what she wanted, too—to be with Eugene forever!

He went on. "I can't wait to laugh and share with you. I see us raising our children here. And our children's children. And celebrating banquets of our own in this very hall for many, many, many, *many* years to come."

The more he talked, the more her smile faded. The things he was saying were nice, but were they what she wanted right now? The feeling of dread got worse as Eugene kept talking.

"I want to ride our horses out to the Corona wall together each and every morning until we

44

are very, *very* old and gray. I love you, Rapunzel. I want to spend the rest of our lives here, together."

That hopeful, positive feeling Rapunzel had when she first saw the ring was fading.

"Here?" She had to be certain that was what he meant. "In this castle forever?"

"I mean, unless you want to rent, but I hardly see how we're going to top this," Eugene joked.

Rapunzel suddenly felt faint. Her head was swimming with Eugene's words, her princess duties, her father's overprotectiveness, and the thought of never leaving the castle. It was all too overwhelming. She lost focus on Eugene and the ring and heard "*this* castle" over and over again.

Then her father's voice was in her head, saying, "Princesses need to be protected at all times."

Rapunzel's eyes regained focus, landing first on the guards at the door, then on the guests at the banquet. She could hear her heart beating in her head as she stared straight ahead, unable to process it all.

"Rapunzel?" Eugene was beginning to feel concerned. "Rapunzel?"

"I—wow—I love you, Eugene, but I can't. Just . . . not now." She turned away from him. "Um, I need some air."

Rapunzel rushed toward the exit, leaving a stunned Eugene in the banquet hall, still on one knee.

chapter

4

It was nighttime in the kingdom. Since the banquet had ended abruptly, Rapunzel and Cassandra were back in Rapunzel's room.

"I feel terrible about Eugene. I—" Rapunzel paced the floor. "I do love him. And I want to marry him someday. But not like this." She was so frustrated. "I need to get out and clear my head *without* a fleet of guards tailing me."

"Say no more," Cassandra said, leading Rapunzel and Pascal to her own room. As the group walked down the corridor and through the main hallway, Rapunzel glanced at all the paintings hanging on the wall. Countless royal images stared back at her. Her mom's portrait stood tall in a golden frame. She wore a long purple gown and a crown atop her head. Then there was her father's portrait. He looked strong and stately with the crest of Corona gleaming from his chest. Between them was a majestic painting of the castle. Rapunzel's home was beautiful. But it was all so new to her. Before she had time to think more, they reached Cassandra's room. Cassandra led Rapunzel and Pascal inside and opened a closet filled with weapons.

Rapunzel gasped. "Whoa. Where's the war?" There were knives of all sizes, crossbows, swords, and even a saw.

"Well, when your dad is captain of the guard, you tend to collect stuff," Cassandra said, changing from her party dress into a more comfortable outfit. When she didn't have lady-in-waiting duties, Cassandra preferred to wear her pants, tunic, and boots—complete with several swords in scabbards.

Rapunzel picked up something that seemed like a normal toy ball, but when she tossed it in the air, sharp spikes burst out of it. Shocked, she put it back and picked up a cloak instead. "I have a feeling this is going to be fun!"

Sliding the hood over her head, Rapunzel looked at Pascal. "Pascal, I need you to stay here and make sure no one knows I'm gone." She had to escape castle life for a little while.

Pascal dutifully saluted her. He took his job seriously.

A short time later, Eugene was walking down the hall toward Rapunzel's door, still dressed in his banquet outfit. He frowned as he passed a portrait of the royal family. How had things gone so wrong? He needed to talk to her.

He was about to enter Rapunzel's room when two guards blocked the way with crossed swords.

"The princess's lady-in-waiting made it

expressly clear that Her Highness does not wish to be disturbed under any circumstances," a guard told him.

"Huh? Lady-in-wai—?" Eugene snorted. "You mean Cassandra? First off, calling Cassandra a 'lady' *anything* is being incredibly generous. Secondly, come on, Stan. It's me, your buddy, Eugene," he said, trying to persuade the guard. "Eugene the fiend! You know Rapunzel would want to talk to me if you let me in."

The guard considered it for a moment, but then said, "Sorry, Eugene. Orders are orders."

"All right, just doing your job. I respect that." Eugene started to leave but turned right back. "You sure there's no way to let me in?"

The guard eyed Eugene's shirt. It was a *really* nice shirt. Stan loved fashion, and Eugene knew it. They both smiled and, without a word, a deal was struck.

Eugene traded his shirt for admission and entered the room wearing just an undershirt. The

room was dark and shadowed, so he didn't see Pascal skitter behind a dressing screen.

"Rapunzel? Rapunzel?" he called into the room.

Pascal couldn't let Eugene know Rapunzel was gone. He turned on a lamp so that only his reflection was visible. He sat atop the bodice of a dress with a potted plant on his head, and his shadow looked so much like the princess that Eugene was fooled into thinking it actually *was* her.

"There you are." Eugene approached the silhouette behind the screen.

"Look, Rapunzel, I'm sorry. I am so sorry. I never should have put you on the spot like that." Eugene went closer. "But I want you to know, I meant it. I want to marry you. I love you."

Pascal was struggling to balance the pot on his head, and it got worse when a fly buzzed nearby. He loved delicious flies.

"It's okay," Eugene continued. "You're still upset. I understand. You're not ready to say it back yet. Totally cool." He turned around and Pascal wiggled toward the fly, making the fake Rapunzel silhouette look as if its arms were waving crazily. Luckily, Eugene didn't see that.

He lay on Rapunzel's bed, forgetting himself for a second. "Oh, *man,* that's a good pillow. What is that? Goose down? Some kind of down." He sniffed it. "Buckwheat husk?"

When Eugene returned his attention to the image of Rapunzel behind the screen, it looked as if she had her hands on her hips. "Sorry." He got serious again. "Look, I know there's still a ton of details we need to figure out . . . and I may have jumped the gun a little." He toyed with the fringe on the pillowcase. "It's just that growing up poor and alone, I got used to having nothing and no one to share it with. But now, with you, I finally have something." The image behind the screen looked as if it were crying, but it was really Pascal wiping his eyes. "*We* have something. Something amazing. And I guess tonight I was just trying to keep it that way. I thought that's what you wanted, too, but maybe I was wrong." Eugene was sad and hurting inside. "Come on, say something!"

Just then, Pascal dropped the potted plant. From the other side of the screen, it looked as if Rapunzel's head had fallen off!

With a shout, Eugene leaped to the screen and pulled it aside to find Pascal sitting on top of the dress form. He gave Eugene a guilty grin.

"Fantastic," Eugene said sarcastically. "I just poured my heart out to a frog." He sighed. "Okay, where did she go?"

The chameleon shrugged.

"Pascal, you do realize that if the king finds out she's gone, we're all going to be in big trouble, right?"

Pascal nodded. Eugene was right—they had to find Rapunzel.

Out in the hall, the guards were chatting as if nothing was wrong. They had no idea the princess was gone.

"I'm aware it's not protocol, Pete," said Stan,

the guard who was wearing Eugene's shirt. "I just happen to think it highlights my mustache."

Eugene opened the door and stepped into the hall with Pascal on his shoulder. "Hey, Stan, great look," he said, commenting on the new outfit as he slipped by both guards. "It really brings out the 'stache!"

Stan gave Pete an "I told you so" look, and Eugene and Pascal bolted out of sight.

Back in the village, Pocket, a sinister crook, called a meeting of Corona's most notorious thieves. He had a job for them. The gathering was held at the thieves' hideout, a cavernous space filled with decayed paintings and crumbling furniture.

One of the thieves stood to the side of the group, painting an apple on a curtain. With an intense stare, Pocket studied the curtain. It would be the perfect disguise for a wagon, which they would need if the thieves accepted the lucrative assignment he was about to explain. Unfortunately, the artistic thief had misspelled "apple," writing "appel" instead, but that wouldn't matter.

The biggest thief slammed his knife into the table. He turned toward Pocket and asked in a threatening voice, "All right, you got us all down here. So what's this plan of yours?"

"It's not my plan, boys. It's Lady Kane's," Pocket told them. He might have arranged everything, but ultimately she was the boss.

The thieves gasped. Lady Kane was a legend. They were impressed.

"Eighteen years ago, the princess was taken from Corona, and it was because of *her* that the king unfairly cracked down on all those he considered *undesirable*—like us."

"Yeah, so?" the big thief asked.

Pocket plucked the man's knife out of the table and carefully ran a finger along the blade. "Lady Kane not only promises to make you all rich, but she's offering you the opportunity to exact revenge on the king *and* his precious little princess."

With a fierce swoosh, Pocket threw the thief's

knife across the room. Everyone ducked as it soared past them and stuck in the wall behind their heads. Pocket grinned. "So who's in?" he asked the group.

When it came to exacting revenge, they were all happy to ruin Rapunzel's coronation.

chapter
5

Cassandra opened a creaky door and entered a dark storage room. Rapunzel followed, wearing a cloak over her head. She tossed back the hood as Cassandra pushed aside a box, then some heavy velvet drapes, to reveal a small tunnel.

Rapunzel couldn't hold in her excitement. "Is that a secret passage?" She accidentally tugged at the drapes, which fell down over Cassandra's head.

"It was until you announced it to the whole castle," Cassandra said, tossing the thick fabric aside to discover that Rapunzel had already gone into the tunnel. "Rapunzel?" She quickly followed the princess.

Moments later, Rapunzel reached the end of

the secret tunnel. She popped a panel out of a grate and emerged at the base of the guard tower.

"That was so fun!" she exclaimed as Cassandra climbed out to join her. They were under the bridge that led to the castle.

"I'd like to take this opportunity to remind you that we're supposed to be *sneaking* out," Cassandra said in a hushed voice as she put the grate cover back in place.

"Cass, I think you'll discover that I can be *pretty* sneaky when I need to—" Rapunzel began, but Cassandra threw herself at Rapunzel, cutting her off and knocking them both into the shadows.

Patrol guards marched past.

Rapunzel let out a long breath. They had almost been caught.

"Nightly patrols," Cassandra explained. "We can get by them if we time it right."

"Wait," Rapunzel asked, "how did you know they were coming?" She watched the guards disappear in the distance.

"I have eyes in the sky." She held out a gloved arm. A majestic owl swooped down and landed on her forearm.

"That's amazing!" Rapunzel gushed. "You have your own owl! What's his name?"

Cassandra rolled her eyes as if that were the silliest question she'd ever heard and answered, "Owl."

She raised her arm and the owl took off into the night sky. Then, with a click of her tongue, Maximus and Fidella slipped out from behind a bunch of barrels.

"Max!" Rapunzel was thrilled to see him.

"When he heard I was sneaking you out of here, he insisted on coming along," Cassandra said, gathering Fidella's reins. "And between you and me, I think he's got something for you-know-who." She nodded toward Fidella.

Max whinnied with embarrassment. Rapunzel rubbed his neck and said in confidence, "It'll be our secret."

The group headed toward the docks. When they reached the shore, Cassandra tied a long rope to an arrow and shot it across the river. The arrow landed near the base of the bridge on the opposite shore. Cassandra and Rapunzel got into a boat with the horses, and then used the rope to pull the boat quietly through the water to the other side.

Back at the castle, Eugene and Pascal were searching everywhere for Rapunzel. Eugene opened a door. "Rapunzel, are you in there?"

Just then, someone cleared their throat. Eugene turned around to find the king approaching him slowly.

"Is who in there, Eugene?" the king asked.

"Huh?" Eugene quickly shut the door and hustled to the king's side. "No one," he said lightly. "This is, uh, just a part of my nightly routine, you know. Oh, yeah, checking the castle for intruders, keeping an eye on Rapunzel like I promised."

The king didn't seem convinced, so Eugene opened the nearest door and shouted into the room, "Hey, is anyone in there?" He paused a beat, then said, "No?" and turned to the king. "Good. See? The system works really well, I think." He knew he sounded foolish, but he couldn't let the king know Rapunzel was missing.

"Eugene," the king said in a firm voice. "Where is Rapunzel?"

"Uh." Eugene and Pascal looked at each other. "In her room, of course." Eugene pointed down the hall.

"Good," the king said, visibly relaxing. "I'd like to speak with her."

"You can't!" Eugene hurried to block his way. He grabbed the king's shoulders, then saw the armed guards nearby and realized grabbing the king was a big mistake. He immediately let go. "I mean, you can, obviously. You can do whatever you want. You're the king. A very large, intimidating, beardy, yet"—Eugene paused, trying to compose himself—"clearly *understanding* king. It's just she's still upset. And she said she needed time alone." The king looked suspiciously over Eugene's shoulder toward Rapunzel's room. "I was only trying to respect that," he rambled on.

King Frederic lowered his eyes at Eugene. It was obvious the king didn't trust him at all.

"But, like I said, you are the king," Eugene continued, sensing the older man's displeasure. "The very sweet and non-hostile king."

The king took one last look at his daughter's door. "Well, maybe she does need time to herself." Eugene breathed a sigh of relief as the king turned to leave. "But when you see her," the king said, "please tell her that I'm looking for her."

There was something else Eugene had to say. He boldly stepped forward. "Sir, about the whole proposal earlier. That didn't go quite as I had hoped."

The king didn't turn around. "We'll discuss

that later, son," he replied, his back to Eugene. "Much later."

"Right," Eugene muttered to himself. He turned to Pascal. "We have bigger fish to fry."

They headed in the opposite direction of the king, hoping they'd find Rapunzel soon.

When the king reached his room, he sat on the edge of his bed staring at a family portrait that hung on the wall. It had been painted right after Rapunzel was born. Things seemed so easy then, so full of promise. That was before she was taken from them and returned as a teenager with her own hopes and dreams. He sighed, letting his shoulders slump.

"Stop beating yourself up, Fred," Queen Arianna told her husband. "Rapunzel just needs some space. Nobody said dealing with teenagers was supposed to be easy." She set the book she was reading aside to give him her full attention.

"Teenager or not, Arianna, she will be queen one day," the king replied. "I have to prepare her for that."

He remembered the night baby Rapunzel was stolen. He could still hear her cries as he called the guards.

The queen came to his side.

"I just want to protect her," the king said, his heart filled with sorrow.

chapter

6

Cassandra and Rapunzel finally made it across the river. Cassandra pulled the barge to shore, and Rapunzel jumped out. They were in a beautiful, lush green forest, looking toward majestic mountains in the distance.

Rapunzel's bare feet touched the soil and she wiggled her toes in cool, soft moss. Her nerves tingled with excitement in anticipation of the adventure that was just beginning.

A light breeze blew, whistling through the trees like a promise.

When Max joined Rapunzel onshore, she gave him a mighty hug. She was about to explore the world and see things she'd only imagined, and she couldn't wait to get started!

The group headed through the moonlit forest into a clearing, where a vast sky filled with stars twinkled down on them. Rapunzel stood still and let the wind blow through her hair. She wanted to absorb everything this moment had to offer.

Seeing the moon's reflection on a tiny pond, Rapunzel danced with joy. It felt so good to be outside and to be free! The fish in the water playfully enticed her, and she followed them along the shore. She jumped when they jumped and ran when they swam.

Soon Rapunzel hopped on Max and they rode through the moonlight, Cassandra and Fidella not far behind. Happiness coursed through her. She'd never felt so carefree. But something made her hesitate. She glanced back the way they'd come, toward the castle. *Will I get in trouble for this?* she wondered. But then she looked ahead again. She needed a break from princess life, and this was her chance to explore.

The two girls rode until they came to a long bridge that spanned a narrow valley.

"There's something I want to show you," Cassandra said, stopping her horse and turning to Rapunzel. "Just remember," she warned. "No one can ever know that I took you outside the walls of Corona."

"Don't worry," Rapunzel assured her. "No one is going to find out!" She spurred Max forward.

Cassandra and Fidella continued along the crumbling bridge. Stones dropped from the bridge into the ravine far below. Max had to move slowly to keep his footing steady. Suddenly, he reared back in fear.

"Whoa, whoa, Max," Rapunzel soothed him. The bridge couldn't hold the horses' weight. "All right, this looks dangerous. Can you stay here and watch Fidella for me?"

The horses agreed to stay near the bridge and wait for Rapunzel and Cassandra to return. The bridge was so fragile, the girls needed to go forward on foot. They were light enough, so they'd be safe.

Once they reached the other side, Rapunzel asked, "So? What did you want to show me?"

"Believe me," Cassandra said as they approached a rocky outcrop. "It's better if you see it for yourself."

Dark crystalline rocks dotted the entire area, growing toward the sky like treacherous spikes.

"They're beautiful," Rapunzel said, taking a closer look. "What are they?"

"Don't know," Cassandra admitted. "They just sprouted up here about a year ago." She drew her sword. "And watch this." She raised her sword to strike. "Uh, you might want to stand back for this one." Cassandra swung with all her strength. The sword shattered.

"Wow," Rapunzel gasped. "They're unbreakable!" She studied a rock formation, walking in a broad circle around it.

"Want to know the weirdest part?" Cassandra asked, pointing at an uprooted plaque in the middle of a crystal crop. The flower seal of Corona

74

Disney
Tangled
The Series

Before Ever After

coronation outfit!

## Rapunzel

The free-spirited, barefoot princess of Corona is back! Now that she's been reunited with her family, she longs to follow her dreams and explore life beyond the castle walls.

# Pascal

Pascal is Rapunzel's loyal pet chameleon. He can often be found on her shoulder or hiding in her hair. He is good friends with Maximus.

Rapunzel's journal!

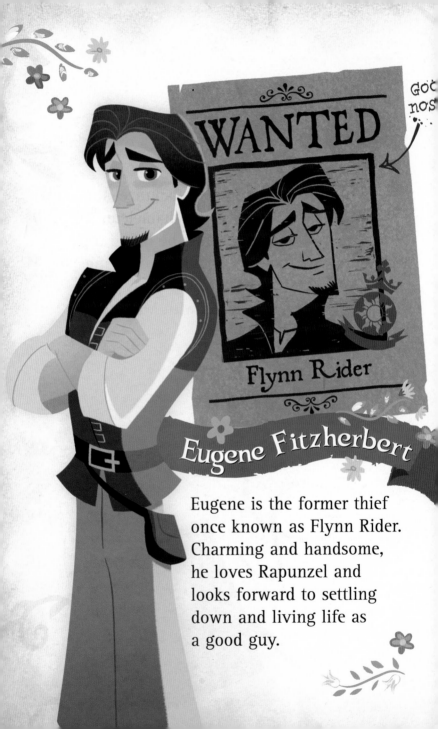

WANTED

Flynn Rider

Goc nos

## Eugene Fitzherbert

Eugene is the former thief
once known as Flynn Rider.
Charming and handsome,
he loves Rapunzel and
looks forward to settling
down and living life as
a good guy.

y-in-waiting
outfit!

Cassandra

Cassandra is Rapunzel's close
friend and lady-in-waiting.
The daughter of the captain
of the guard, she is a skilled
fighter who dreams of joining
the royal guard.

# Captain of the Guard

As the leader of the royal guard, Cassandra's father is in charge of keeping the kingdom safe. Loyal and strong, he is always watching out for the royal family.

## Maximus

Maximus is daring, brave, and devoted to protecting his friends and the kingdom of Corona. But the sweet-natured Rapunzel can always penetrate his tough exterior.

loves apples!

# King Frederic

The king is fiercely protective of Rapunzel, and he loves his daughter dearly. He'll do anything to make sure she is safe.

# Queen Arianna

Graceful and kind, Rapunzel's mother shares her daughter's free spirit. She understands Rapunzel's need to become her own person.

Often found here!

The SNUGGLY DUCKLING

## Pub Thugs

This group of friendly ruffians always has Rapunzel's back. There's Ulf, the mime; Attila, a budding baker; Shorty, the oldest of the group; Vladimir, a lover of unicorns; Big Nose, the ultimate romantic; and Hook Foot, who dreams of becoming a dancer.

was clearly etched into the metal. "This is where they found the miracle flower that saved your mom."

Rapunzel bent down toward the spot. "And me," she added in a whisper.

They were at the site of the legendary magical flower that had healed Queen Arianna, given Rapunzel her power, and bestowed eternal youth on Mother Gothel.

There was a marker nearby. Rapunzel reached toward the plaque, and the surrounding rocks began to glow. Entranced, she reached farther to touch the closest one, careful to avoid the spiked tip.

The instant Rapunzel touched the crystal, the glow intensified. The glow grew brighter and brighter until the crystal exploded in a powerful blast that sent the girls flying backward. When the explosion settled, Rapunzel and Cassandra were lying on the ground, stunned.

Luckily, no one had been hurt. But Rapunzel

soon noticed a shocking sight: one lock of her brown hair had turned blond, the same color it had been before Eugene cut it.

There was no time to absorb this new development. Sharp crystals began to sprout from the ground. More and more of them angrily burst upward, their razor-sharp points glinting in the moonlight. The crystals moved toward the girls, pushing them backward as if chasing them.

The girls staggered to their feet and began to run. With each step they took, the spiked crystals followed, moving closer and closer.

"Wait, what is—" Rapunzel began, but Cassandra cut her off.

"Get to the horses as fast as you can and don't look back!" she shouted.

They passed through a steep valley, and the spiked crystals erupted out of the sides of the mountain. The girls ducked in time, but the spikes narrowly missed their heads.

"Don't stop, Rapunzel! Keep going!" Cassandra

cried. She kicked some rocks toward the crystals in the hope that they would slow them down.

On her own now, Rapunzel jumped off a small ledge and headed toward the bridge where they had left the horses. She was almost there when she realized there was a problem.

A *big* problem.

"Um, Cassandra!" Rapunzel called over her shoulder.

"Keep moving! We need to—" Cassandra froze in her tracks when she saw the princess. "Whoa!"

Rapunzel's blond hair was back—all seventy feet of it.

"What happened?" Cassandra gasped.

"I have no idea!" Rapunzel held a long lock of hair in her hand. She couldn't believe what she was seeing. Then she heard the crystals popping through the ground, coming closer by the second. "But we'll have to deal with it later." She grabbed Cassandra's hand. "Let's go!"

They made it to the bridge. The horses were

close, but the crystals were coming faster than they could run. Max stepped forward, eager to help. A large piece of the bridge crumbled beneath his hooves, leaving a huge gap. The entire bridge began to shake.

Cassandra and Rapunzel fell. They managed to get up and start running again, but Rapunzel's hair snagged on part of the crumbling bridge.

"Cassandra—my hair!" she shouted. Rapunzel pulled and pulled, but it was no use. She was stuck!

Cassandra ran back to help, but they couldn't pull Rapunzel free. The crystals crashed into the bridge, causing the entire structure to shake violently. Cassandra tried to cut Rapunzel's hair with a new sword, but the hair was too strong.

Suddenly, the bridge dropped. Rapunzel held on to her trapped hair and Cassandra held on to Rapunzel, but they were being dragged down toward the ravine.

Max leaped over the break in the bridge and stomped on the place where Rapunzel's hair was caught. The area shattered, and Rapunzel's hair was free.

But the girls were still hanging dangerously from what remained of the bridge. As the spikes continued to burst through the mountainside and fill the ravine, Max leaped toward Rapunzel and Cassandra. At the same time, both girls jumped toward him. Rapunzel landed safely on his back, but Cassandra missed. She clung to the edge of the ravine, sliding off as the bridge crumbled behind her.

"Cassandra!" Rapunzel shouted.

In a heartbeat, Fidella grabbed the back of Cassandra's tunic with her teeth and pulled her to the top of the ravine. They were safe at last.

"See?" Cassandra joked. "I told you I'd get you in and out without anyone knowing." She dusted herself off. "Piece of cake."

"Piece of cake?" Rapunzel cried. "Did you see the seventy feet of hair growing from my head? My father's going to kill me!"

"One problem at a time, please," Cassandra said.

First, they had to get back inside the castle. Then they could figure out what to do about Rapunzel's hair.

chapter

7

As the sun began to rise, Rapunzel and Cassandra peered through a back entrance to the castle.

"We've got a problem," Cassandra said. "Because of the coronation, they've doubled security at the gates today."

"And there's no other way in?" Rapunzel asked. She tightened her cloak around her head, but there was no hiding all that hair.

"Sure, if you want to walk through the front door in broad daylight," Cassandra told her.

Rapunzel looked up to a tall tower above them. Her room was in the tower. "Hmm," she said. "Maybe we don't need the front door."

The girls quickly came up with a new plan. Leaving Fidella with Rapunzel and Cassandra, Max went into the castle to create a distraction. He crept down the hallway toward Rapunzel's room and stopped before the guards, looking at each of them intently.

"Uh, sir," Stan said in response to Max's look. It wasn't unusual for Max to be in the castle. He was an important part of Rapunzel's guard, after all. "I am happy to say all is well and there is nothing to report," Stan continued.

Max eyed the guard's new shirt. "I told him it wasn't protocol, sir," Pete said, pointing at Stan.

Max sent the two guards away with a snort and entered Rapunzel's room.

Just then, a long lock of Rapunzel's blond hair flipped through the window. Max grabbed it and held on tightly. Cassandra used the hair rope to climb in, then she and Max pulled Rapunzel and the rest of her hair inside.

Seeing that her charges were all right, Fidella

returned to the stables, knowing the mission was complete.

But now that they were back safe and sound, Rapunzel was frantic. "Okay, quick. Hand me those scissors!" She wanted her long hair gone—immediately.

Cassandra grabbed the scissors from a nearby table. "So . . . what do we want to do here?" she asked, imitating a hairdresser. "A bob? How about some layers?"

"Just cut it!" Rapunzel was desperate. They had to hurry!

Cassandra tried to cut the thick blond hair, but the scissors shattered! "Uh-oh," she said.

Rapunzel tried to peer behind her. "Uh-oh? Why *uh-oh*? There shouldn't be any uh-ohs!"

Cassandra showed Rapunzel the shattered scissors. "Uh-oh," the princess muttered.

"Was your hair always this strong?" Cassandra asked.

"What?" Rapunzel was baffled. "No. Try again."

Cassandra tried a knife. It bent.

"We're going to need a plan B," Rapunzel said.

Cassandra grabbed a satchel of tools from Max's saddle and picked out a cleaver. She spread Rapunzel's hair out on a long wooden table and prepared to swing. "Cover your eyes!" she shouted.

CRASH! The cleaver shattered.

Cassandra tried a battle-axe, a scythe, and Rapunzel's frying pan. But nothing worked, and soon the wooden table had broken into two large pieces. She collapsed, exhausted. "Forget it," she said at last. "It's just like those stupid rocks. It's unbreakable!"

"We can't forget it!" Rapunzel was horrified. "Today is my coronation!"

The girls were interrupted by a knock on the door.

"Hey, sunshine, are you in there?" It was Eugene. Sitting on his shoulder, Pascal clicked his tongue, as if to say, "Let us in."

Rapunzel moved toward the door, but Cassandra

grabbed her. "You can't let Eugene see you," she warned.

Rapunzel didn't understand. "What? Why?"

"He can't know *anything* about last night!" Cassandra said. "I told you—if it gets out that I took you outside Corona, I'm done for."

"But I trust Eugene." Rapunzel couldn't imagine not telling him.

"Well, I don't," Cassandra replied harshly. "My dad will have me taken off princess detail! We'll never see each other again."

Conflicted, Rapunzel eyed Cassandra. She didn't know what to do when again, Eugene's voice came through the door. "Oh, come on. We've been looking for you all night."

Rapunzel gave Cassandra a look that shouted "Help!" as the two of them scrambled to hide Rapunzel's hair.

"Hey, are you okay in there?" Eugene shouted. "I can hear you, you know."

Rapunzel's hair got caught on something. She squealed from the pain.

Outside, Eugene was beginning to panic. "Rapunzel? Rapunzel!"

Inside, Rapunzel and Cassandra were stuffing all seventy feet of Rapunzel's hair into every available hiding place. Rapunzel pushed some into the closet. Cassandra shoved some under the bed. Max hid a lump under the rug.

"Rapunzel!" Eugene couldn't take it anymore. He was too worried. "Stand back!" he warned.

POW! He kicked in the door.

"Are you—" Eugene stopped when he saw the hair all over the room.

There was hardly an inch of space that didn't have long blond hair stuffed in it. Even the potted plant was hanging from a braided hair holder.

*"Holy hair!"* Eugene exclaimed.

Rapunzel, Cassandra, and Max froze. Pascal was the only one thrilled to have Rapunzel's old look back.

Rapunzel gave Eugene a small smile. "Surprise," she said.

chapter

8

Eugene paced Rapunzel's room, rambling nervously. "Okay, this is new. I mean, no—not new, because we've seen blond hair before. Obviously, that whole magic thing is involved again. It *is* magic, right?" He sat down in a large stuffed chair.

Behind him, Cassandra was piling Rapunzel's hair up at her feet.

"Actually, you don't need to tell me," Eugene continued. "I'll just go ahead and say your hair magically grew back—I'm not going to ask *how*. Obviously, you don't want to tell me, or you wouldn't have tried to hide it. So I won't ask how it grew back, but tell me, please, how did it grow back?" He stood up. "Don't answer that. The important thing is you're okay. You are okay, right?" He sat back down. "Because as long as you're okay, I don't care what happened. I mean, I care, of course I care, but I'm sure there's a reasonable explanation."

"Thank you for understanding," said Rapunzel.

"Oh, come on! Really?" exclaimed Eugene. He wasn't understanding this at all. "I thought we trusted each other, Rapunzel!"

"We do!" Rapunzel replied. "I do. It's just—"

Eugene cut her off. "Fine!" He held up his hands in surrender. "You know what? I can't make you tell me what happened, but obviously you're keeping *something* from me. But whatever it is, I just want you to know, you should never feel like you have to hide anything."

Rapunzel, Max, and Pascal smiled. Cassandra frowned.

Eugene stepped forward and faced Rapunzel.

"You don't hide things from the people you love," he continued. "Ever."

Just then, the queen called out from the hall-way. "Rapunzel!"

Eugene immediately changed his mind. *"Hide your hair!"* he shouted frantically. "Woman, you've got to hide your hair!"

"Rapunzel, may I come in?" the queen asked. She pushed the door open slightly, and Pascal shoved it closed. Max stood on his hind legs and pressed his back against the door to help keep it shut.

"You can't!" Rapunzel shouted, pretending her mouth was full. "I'm brushing my teeth."

"Oh, well, good," her mother said. "I can still come in, though, can't I?"

"Believe me, Mom," Rapunzel shouted through the closed door, "you don't want to. Morning breath. I wouldn't want to expose you to that." She gave a thumbs-up to Eugene and Cassandra.

They looked at her as if to say, *Really? That's*

*the best you could come up with?* Rapunzel shrugged. She didn't have a better idea.

"Uh, that's very thoughtful of you," the queen said, clearly confused. "Daddy and I want you to join us on the terrace for breakfast."

"I don't know," Rapunzel replied. "There's a lot of stuff I have to do to get ready." She held a huge pile of hair in her hands. What was she going to do with it all?

"Daddy has something very important to share with you. He's been waiting all night," the queen told her.

Rapunzel had no choice. "Yeah. Sure. Uh, I'll meet you there in a minute," she replied.

Satisfied, the queen nodded and walked away.

"The coronation is in two hours!" Rapunzel cried. "How am I supposed to cut this hair?"

Cassandra looked at Pascal and Max leaning against the bedroom door. The way they stood, Max's tail rested on Pascal's head. Cassandra studied them for a moment. "I might have an idea," she said.

Below Rapunzel's tower, guests were already arriving for the coronation. Out in the village, castle guards were carefully inspecting the food carts and catering wagons that were entering through a city gate.

A guard stopped one of the wagons. "Hold it. What's in the cart?"

An older, bearded man raised a pie toward him. "Supplies for the coronation," he said. The cart had a painted curtain on it that read APPEL PIES. "Apple" was misspelled.

The guard opened the back of the wagon to double-check. Inside were bags of apples and boxes of butter, ingredients for the pies. It looked all right.

"Very good, move along," he said, waving the wagon forward.

"Thank you, General." The old man gave the guard a pie.

Once the wagon had passed the guard, Lady

Kane's thieves emerged from the shadows. The wagon was merely a decoy and their ticket into Corona. Pocket led the way and the thieves snuck into the back of the wagon.

"Okay, boys. Time to go to work," Pocket said as they prepared to cause trouble.

In a beautiful gazebo on the castle lawn, Rapunzel ate breakfast with her parents.

"So, Rapunzel, ready for the big day?" The queen tried to sound normal, but she and the king were staring at Rapunzel's head in shock.

Rapunzel was wearing a gigantic wig that refused to stay in place. She leaned left, then right, then left again to keep it from toppling over.

"You bet." Rapunzel pointed to the wig. "See? Already in the princess spirit. The bigger the wig, the better the princess, right?" That was sort of what the Duchess of Quintonia had said when she'd first arrived. The wig slid forward, and

Rapunzel quickly pushed it back on her head. "So, Dad, Mom said you wanted to talk?"

"Yes, Rapunzel," the king replied. "Last night, your mother and I had a discussion." He stood as he gathered his thoughts. "I know that I'm not always able to separate the man from the king. Separating the *father* from the king has proven even more difficult."

King Frederic looked at his wife, who encouraged him to continue while Rapunzel rebalanced her wig.

"Sweetheart, I know this new life is hard to get used to. And I'm sure sometimes you wish I would just get out of your hair."

Hair! The irony made Rapunzel choke. "Sorry," she said, touching her throat. "It's a little dry out here. Anyone else dry?"

The king reached out and took her hands in his. "Rapunzel, you're going to be queen someday. A great queen, in fact. Now, you know better than anyone else what a dangerous and evil place the world can be. Not only do I want to keep you safe from that danger and evil, but I must also make sure you are prepared to face them as a leader when the time comes."

The king looked earnestly at his daughter and then continued. "It wasn't until last night that I realized my methods at times may seem strict or unfair."

"Does this mean I can have more time to myself without having half the royal guard looking over my shoulder?" Rapunzel asked hopefully.

"It means I'm willing to reconsider those methods. But I make no promises," the king replied.

Rapunzel knew it was as close to a compromise as he would give her. "I can work with that," she said, smiling.

As Rapunzel kissed her father's cheek, her wig wobbled and a long strand of blond hair slipped free. She quickly crammed it back under the wig and got up from the breakfast table.

"Well, I have to go," she said. "I have a lot of princessing up to do."

The king and queen watched as Rapunzel dashed inside, struggling to keep her wig balanced.

"You're right, Arianna," the king said with a sigh. "Teenagers are a whole new frontier."

Meanwhile, Pocket and his band of thieves had made it into the village and were ready to put their plan into action.

Two thieves approached a glass vendor. They flipped his cart, shattering the trinkets, then stole his money. Guards swooped in, and the duo was immediately arrested.

Another thief robbed the village bank. The people inside fearfully ran out of the building. When the guards arrived, the thief was carrying two giant bags of coins. The bags were bursting at the seams, and some of the coins fell out and clinked against the floor. The thief put down the money he'd stolen and raised his hands in surrender.

Pocket, the ringleader, threw a brick through the jewelry store window and took the largest diamond. Max, who was on duty, immediately caught him and turned him over to the guards.

Once all the thieves had been rounded up, the royal guards threw them into a wagon and took them to the castle's dungeon.

Little did the guards know, this was exactly what the thieves had planned. All they had to do next was wait for Lady Kane.

In the castle wardrobe room, Cassandra made the final adjustments to Rapunzel's dress for the coronation.

Eugene popped his head into the room. "How are you?" he asked.

Cassandra gave him a look, then went back to sewing.

"Oh, come on," he begged. "What's going on with Rapunzel? I mean, is it something I did?" Why wouldn't Rapunzel tell him how her blond hair had grown back? Pascal sat on the window seat as Eugene began to pace.

Cassandra didn't look up from her work. "Probably."

Eugene stared at her for a moment. "And since when did she start keeping secrets from me?" he asked.

"Hey, Fitzherbert," Cassandra said. "I need to get this done before the coronation, so do you mind throwing your pity party someplace else?" She continued stitching the dress sleeve she was holding.

"Look, *Cassandra*, I know you don't like me for Rapunzel—"

"That's not true. I don't like you for anyone," she told him, finishing her work.

"I just want what's best for her," he said.

"You don't say." Cassandra rolled her eyes.

"Of course! I want her to feel safe," he responded, frustrated. "I want her to be taken care of. And I want her to be happy here."

Cassandra rose. "Funny," she said, "you seem to have a pretty good handle on the things *you* want." She left and slammed the door shut behind her.

Eugene sat down and looked at Pascal, who clearly thought Cassandra was right.

"Oh, don't you start," he said, shaking his head.

Rapunzel was in her room, about to remove her wig, when there was a knock at the door.

"Hi, honey," the queen said, popping her head in.

"Oh, hi, Mom," Rapunzel greeted her, readjusting the giant wig on her head.

"You left so quickly after breakfast, I didn't have the chance to give you this." The queen sat next to Rapunzel on her bed and held out a simple wooden box. "I know it's a little early for a coronation gift, but I thought you might like to see it now."

Rapunzel opened the box and found a journal inside. She flipped eagerly through the pages, reading snippets of entries.

"'Eighteenth of July,'" Rapunzel read aloud. "'We embarked on a safari to the most remote

plains of the third continent. Twenty-first of May: had to take shelter in a hidden cave to escape the fury of a violent storm. Twelfth of April: helped villagers rebuild their war-torn homes.'" Rapunzel looked into the queen's eyes. "Mom, is this yours? Did you actually *do* all these things?"

"Rapunzel, before I met your dad, I was so much like you," the queen said. "I had no idea what I was supposed to do in this world. So I went out and found my own way."

The queen reached into the box and pulled out another journal. This one was blank. She looked intently at her daughter and then said, "Dad is right about one thing: you'll be queen someday. But only you get to decide what kind of queen you'll be. And *no one* can tell you the best way to make that decision."

Rapunzel clutched the blank journal. "Are you suggesting that I should—"

The queen put out a hand to stop her from saying anything more. "Find a way to fill these pages," she said. "I only ask that you be safe, smart, and above all else, true to yourself."

Rapunzel turned to the first page of the journal, where her mother had written an inscription:

*Plus est en vous —Your Mother*

*"Plus est en vous?"* asked Rapunzel.

"It means 'There is more in you,'" said the queen.

Hearing those words brought a rush of happiness and love to Rapunzel. Maybe her mother understood her more than she knew. She wrapped her mom in a huge hug.

chapter

9

The coronation was about to begin. The guests were all seated in the castle's royal throne room. The king and queen stood at the end of a long aisle, awaiting Rapunzel's grand entrance. The official princess crown was perched on a velvet cushion between them.

Rapunzel was in her dressing room, adjusting the wig. It towered high above her and was the same shade of pink as her dress. And while the wig was big, Rapunzel's dress was bigger. It was the most ornate outfit Rapunzel had ever seen. Soft pink fabric jutted far out to each side, creating a beautiful, flowing ball gown. The bodice was a corset of gold with an intricate design woven into it. And her shoulders had puffed sleeves in stripes of lilac and gold.

But Cassandra only had eyes for hiding Rapunzel's real hair. "This would have been so much easier with the other girls helping, but they're such gossips, half the kingdom would know about your hair by now," Cassandra said as she shoved Rapunzel's hair under the wig. Blond strands popped out left and right.

"Are you sure you can't see it?" Rapunzel asked.

"Positive," Cassandra replied, putting Rapunzel's high collar in place to cover the last few strands at her neck. "Are you sure you can pull this off?"

Rapunzel peered out the side door at her father. He was beaming with pride as he waited for the coronation to begin. She couldn't disappoint him.

"I have to, Cassandra," she said.

"Just be careful you don't trip," Cassandra said, adjusting Rapunzel's gown.

"It's not the dress I'm worried about," Rapunzel said, pulling up the hem to reveal a pair of

high-heeled shoes. "How do people walk in these things?"

Cassandra helped steady her. "Just relax. It's going to be fine. Are you ready for your big entrance?"

Rapunzel nodded, knocking her wig off slightly.

"You can do this, Rapunzel," Cassandra assured her, fixing the wig one last time. "Just don't make any sudden movements." She ushered the soon-to-be-princess out the door and toward the throne room's entrance.

Rapunzel took a deep breath. "Okay." She nodded to Cassandra, who signaled for the guards to open the doors.

Rapunzel's eyes grew wide as she took in the crowd of people inside the throne room. The music began and the crowd rose to their feet. Everyone was staring at her. The king and queen beamed from the far end of the hall.

When Eugene saw Rapunzel in her gown, the light streaming from behind her, all he could say was "Wow."

Rapunzel took her first step forward. This was really happening. She was about to officially be crowned a princess. All she had to do was walk to the end of the aisle. But getting there was harder than it seemed. In her high-heeled shoes, she felt as if she were walking on a high-wire. "Whoa, whoa," she repeated with each wobbly step.

When the music ended, the crowd exchanged nervous glances. Rapunzel wasn't at the end of the aisle yet. She smiled and continued her slow wobble, desperate not to fall. The room was awkwardly silent.

"*How* embarrassing for her," said the Duchess of Quintonia, wearing her own tall wig. "This is going to take forever." She quietly slipped out of the throne room and made her way to the castle dungeon, an evil glint in her eye. Her ornate fan opened to reveal a map of the most direct route.

When she reached the guarded cell where the thieves were being held, she pretended to be lost.

"Hello? Can anyone help me?" she called out,

approaching the guards. "I must have taken a wrong turn somewhere."

One of the guards left his post. "I'll be glad to help you, madame."

"Oh, you're too kind."

Suddenly, the duchess attacked, using her fan as a weapon. With amazing skill, she managed to take down both guards in seconds. She found the keys to the cell on a nearby hook, just as she'd expected.

"Hey, Madame Poppycock, the party's upstairs," a large thief said, mocking her dress and wig. He didn't know who this woman was, but he was about to find out.

She grabbed him through the bars and slammed his head into the wall.

Pocket rose from a bench. "Meet Lady Kane," he told the others.

The big thief was suddenly scared. "You're a lot stronger than you look," he admitted.

"I'm a lot of things." Lady Kane took off her

wig and sneered, then opened the prison door. "Let the show begin."

Just as the thieves were walking out of the cell, a castle guard arrived, his weapon drawn.

"I'm going to need you to step back into that cell, pronto," he said.

Lady Kane moved forward and was immediately surrounded by the criminals.

The big guy cracked his knuckles. "That there is a nice suit," he told the guard, referring to his armor.

Outnumbered, the guard dropped his weapon and surrendered.

The thieves stole his suit and hurried out of the dungeon.

Back in the throne room, Rapunzel had finally made it to the end of the aisle without falling. The bishop began the coronation service.

"The wearer of this crown," he announced, "is a shining example of the promise that is Corona.

An ambassador of goodwill to those visiting from afar."

Rapunzel adjusted her wig and gave Eugene a thumbs-up. So far, so good.

"And an inspiration to those fortunate enough to live within her borders," the bishop continued.

Eugene gave Rapunzel a thumbs-up back.

Cassandra found her seat, Pascal on her shoulder, as the bishop went on. "But above all, the chief responsibility of the crown is to keep the people of Corona safe from dangers near and far."

Pascal noticed an unfamiliar guard enter the room and lock the back door. He tapped his tail on Cassandra's cheek to get her attention.

"And there are many," said the bishop.

Cassandra saw guards entering from all sides of the room. Like Pascal, she didn't recognize any of them. It didn't take her long to realize that these men weren't castle guards.

"Go find Max," Cassandra whispered urgently to Pascal.

"There will come a day when the walls that

surround Corona are threatened by maleficence," continued the bishop.

Cassandra caught Eugene's eye. He had noticed the fake guards, too.

The bishop raised the princess's crown. "A day—"

"Attention, please!" a woman interrupted from the back of the room.

Eugene recognized the voice from his own days as a thief. "Lady Kane?" he said in surprise.

Lady Kane's band of villains drew their swords and forced the highest-ranking royal guests to kneel. Frightened people ran for the exits, but all the doors were locked.

Eugene backed into the shadows, watching the situation unfold and waiting for the right moment to act.

"Release my guests immediately!" the king demanded.

Lady Kane stormed toward him. "What's the matter, Fred? Am I ruining your little girl's perfect day?"

114

Rapunzel stood near her parents. "Duchess?" she asked in confusion.

"Oh, honey, I am *no* duchess," Lady Kane replied.

"I don't understand," said Rapunzel.

"Of course you wouldn't, *Rapunzel*," Lady Kane jeered. She brought her face inches from Rapunzel's. "But understand this: this is all your fault!"

"What?" Rapunzel asked.

Lady Kane grasped Rapunzel's shoulders. "You see, after your untimely disappearance, your father locked up every criminal in the kingdom." She moved to face the king. "Including a simple petty thief." She touched the medallion that hung around the king's neck, then turned toward Rapunzel. "My father," she sneered. "I saw him thrown into a cage and hauled off like some animal—never to be seen again." She pulled out her sword and walked in front of her royal prisoners. "So I thought I'd come back and return the favor!" Her expression was pure evil as she pointed her sword at the king.

Just then, one of the thieves wheeled the apple

pie wagon in through a side door. The sign fell to reveal a jailer's wagon.

"Load 'em up, boys," Lady Kane told her crew.

The royal guests and castle guards climbed into the wagon, their heads hanging low. Once they were all inside, Lady Kane turned to the king. "Your turn, Your Majesty."

The king pushed Rapunzel and the queen behind him.

"Oh, come on, you didn't think we'd leave our fattest pig in the pen, did you?" Lady Kane snickered.

Two dangerous thieves dragged the king to the wagon.

"Dad!" Rapunzel called out.

"Rapunzel, stay back," the king warned her.

"But—"

"No!" he shouted. "There is nothing you can do. As your father and your king, I command you to stay put!"

The wagon door shut with a bang.

chapter

10

Almost all the royal guests were now trapped inside the wagon. But a few people were still free—including Rapunzel, Eugene, and Cassandra. Eugene stepped forward but was immediately blocked by two goons with swords. "Don't be a hero, pretty boy," one warned.

Eugene looked from Rapunzel to Cassandra. They both knew what he was thinking and nodded.

"Sorry, Dad," said Rapunzel. "I have to do this."

"Rapunzel! No!" the king shouted as Rapunzel kicked off her uncomfortable shoes and tore off her wig. She shook her head, and her long blond hair tumbled down around her feet.

"That's my girl!" said Eugene.

Rapunzel stepped forward. "Let them go!" Her hair glowed with power, like the magical sundrop flower that had created it.

"It's amazing what you can hide under a wig, isn't it, Princess?" Lady Kane laughed and turned to her thieves. "Come on. Let's move out!" She jumped on the side of the wagon, ready to make her getaway.

"Hi-yah!" Rapunzel whipped her hair across the hall. It snared the wagon door and tore it from its hinges.

Lady Kane leaped down from the wagon. "Oh, now you're just making me angry."

"Good. I'm just getting started," Rapunzel replied, pulling back her hair and readying herself for battle.

The royal captives quickly climbed out of the wagon.

"Get those people back here! Now!" Lady Kane screeched.

The king rushed to his daughter, shouting, "Rapunzel, your hair!"

"I know," she told him. "We'll talk about it later." She helped a woman cross the room, then turned back to him. "Please get somewhere safe, and take care of Mom. I've got this!"

"Rapunzel!" the king called out, but quickly realized he couldn't stop her.

Eugene was standing between Pocket and another goon. "That's my cue," he said, and slammed their heads together—hard. The two men fell to the ground.

"Well, it's my last day on princess duty," Cassandra muttered. She grabbed a candelabra and jumped into the fray. "I might as well go down fighting."

The thieves cornered the royal guests. One held out a menacing weapon.

"Leave them alone." Rapunzel tossed a strand

of hair and lassoed the weapon, then wrapped the thief in her hair like a mummy and toppled him to the ground.

The king moved forward to fight with his daughter. But he was stopped by a hand on his shoulder. He turned around to see his wife looking intently at him.

"Just wait," said the queen.

Eugene and Cassandra were fighting back to back.

"So, you sure you can handle yourself?" Eugene teased her.

"Oh, I'll manage," Cassandra replied. She broke off the candles from the candelabra, creating a fighting stick with the holder just as a thief came running at her. Using her new weapon as a staff, she knocked the goon off his feet, then deftly took down a second.

Eugene battled two thieves on his own, holding them off with a sword. He swiftly disarmed one of the bandits before using his sword to knock down another. Then he got down on one knee, preparing to face a third.

Suddenly, the doors to the throne room shook as real castle guards tried to break in.

"Get those doors open now!" the captain of the guard shouted to his men. They hefted a battering ram into position and prepared to break down the doors.

Two of Lady Kane's men were closing in on a few of the royal guests. Rapunzel swung her hair over the rafters to catch them by their waists. Then she jumped down, and the men went flying up to the rafters and out of the fight.

Cassandra faced Lady Kane, who was armed with a sword, while Cassandra still held the candelabra as a staff.

Lady Kane looked at Cassandra's weapon. "Cute," she snorted, then knocked Cassandra to the ground. When Cassandra got up, Lady Kane whipped out two of her fans and swiped them dangerously at her.

On the other side of the room, Rapunzel swung around on a strand of her long hair and knocked down two thieves. When one caught hold of her hair, she used another strand to grab the best weapon she could: a frying pan. She tore it from the side of the wagon and aimed it for the thief's head. A loud *bong* echoed through the room, and the guy crashed to the ground.

Rapunzel then flung the frying pan to Eugene, who had just been disarmed.

"Thanks, Blondie!" he said, tossing it like a boomerang and knocking out three bad guys. "Now, this feels good!"

Rapunzel and Eugene had defeated most of the thieves, but Cassandra was still battling Lady Kane. The woman was a wicked opponent, but Cassandra finally managed to knock her to the ground.

"Stay down!" she demanded, pinning Lady Kane to the floor. Rapunzel hurried over to help her friend.

"You have no idea who you're dealing with," Lady Kane growled at Rapunzel.

"Believe me, I've dealt with much worse," Rapunzel replied.

Suddenly, Lady Kane freed herself from Cassandra's grasp and did a series of backflips to the throne room door. She grabbed the battle-axe that was holding the door shut.

"You think this is over?" she sneered. "I promise you, I'll be back." She ripped off the door handle just as Max and the royal guards broke the doors down.

Lady Kane was instantly crushed and pinned to the ground. She whimpered from beneath the rubble.

It *was* over. The three friends—Rapunzel, Cassandra, and Eugene—stood proudly together. Around them, the royal guests clapped and cheered.

The guards rushed inside and quickly handcuffed and ushered out Lady Kane and her thieves.

Eugene gave a twirl of the frying pan, and Maximus let out a happy and satisfied whinny.

Rapunzel glanced up just in time to see her mother rush toward her with a giant smile on her face. Queen Arianna wrapped her daughter in a huge embrace.

Thanks to Rapunzel and her friends, everyone was safe.

chapter

11

After Lady Kane and her thieves had been taken away and all the guests had left, Rapunzel went to see her father in the now-empty throne room. He sat in his high-backed chair, deep in thought. She stood before him, feeling small and a little afraid. Then she began to tell him her story.

"So, I am trying to understand this," the king said, speaking slowly. "You snuck out last night and went beyond the walls of Corona, where you touched a mysterious rock that somehow caused your hair to return?"

"Yes," Rapunzel replied.

"And you acted alone?"

Rapunzel avoided the question. "Look, I know you're angry. But can't you see? I'm okay. I'm more than okay, actually. I—"

"Rapunzel," the king interrupted. "There is something I need to tell you." He rose from his throne and came down to stand next to her. "The night you were taken, a part of me died. The best part of me. For eighteen long and agonizing years, I swore that if somehow, some way, by some *miracle,* the fates decided to show mercy and return you to me, I would never let anything happen to you again."

He reached out to take a lock of Rapunzel's hair between his fingers.

"And now that this has returned—the very reason you were snatched away from me in the first place—I'm afraid I'm left with no choice, sweetheart." He turned away from her, refusing to look at her any longer. "As of tonight, I am forced to exercise my martial right as king to forbid you to leave the walls of this kingdom without my consent."

"Father." Rapunzel stepped forward, ready to plead with him.

"And know this," the king went on, taking her crown from a nearby stand and handing it to her. "This is the last we'll speak of mystical rocks or magic of any kind. To anyone. Is that understood?"

Rapunzel's eyes filled with tears as she took the crown. Why couldn't her father understand her? Didn't he know what she was capable of? "There is so much more to me than you think," she said. Then she ran out of the room.

Back in her bedroom, Rapunzel turned to the one thing that had always cheered her up: painting. She sat on her window seat, Pascal on her shoulder, and painted the events of the last few days in her new journal.

There was a knock on the door, and Eugene poked his head in. He held a tray in one hand, and a towel hung from his arm. "I believe somebody ordered room service?" He presented Rapunzel with a cupcake like the one from town that she had never gotten to eat.

"Eugene!" Rapunzel was happy to see him. Just by being there, he cheered her up right away. "How did you know?"

Eugene shrugged. "Had a feeling." Then he grew serious. "Look, I wanted to clear up some stuff." He sat with her on the window seat and handed over the cupcake. "I haven't had the chance to apologize for putting you on the spot with my proposal."

Rapunzel set the cupcake aside. "Looking back, storming out of the room probably wasn't the *best* reaction." She sighed. "I'm sorry."

"No," he protested. "No. Don't apologize. I'll admit, I don't quite understand why you said no." He reached out to take her hands in his. "But I promise to do everything I can until I do."

Rapunzel looked into his eyes. "Thanks, Eugene."

"And in the meantime, we'll stay right here and take things slowly." He lifted a lock of her hair. "I miss this."

"Hey, promise me one more thing," she said.

"Anything," he told her.

"That you'll be patient with me."

"Absolutely." He leaned in and kissed her, then pulled back and rested his forehead on hers. "Good night, Rapunzel."

"Good night, Eugene," she replied as she watched him leave.

Alone, Rapunzel considered what happily-ever-after really meant. She was back to being stuck inside the castle. Sure, she had people around her who loved her, but would it ever be enough? Had she left one tower only to be stuck in another?

The wind blew through her open window, riffling the blank pages of her journal. She saw the inscription her mother had written:

*Plus est en vous. —Your Mother*

133

A spark lit inside Rapunzel. She stepped out onto the terrace and looked down at Corona. There was so much more in this world to see. Rapunzel promised herself she wouldn't miss another moment. And there was so much more inside her, waiting to be discovered.

This was just the beginning.